Available Books:

Melvin Goes to School
Melvin Rides The Bus

TINY HOUSE PUBLISHING (USA) LLC
4 Wexford Drive, Chichester, NH 03258

Tiny House
Publishing

Graphic design by Dennis Schaefer – www.dschaeferdesign.com

Body text set in 12-point Kristen ITC.
Survival Guide and Survival Kit text in back set in 13-point Kristen ITC.

ISBN (paperback): 978-0-9967270-6-8
ISBN (ebook): 978-0-9967270-7-5

Disclaimer

Melvin is intended to be a character that all children can relate to. We understand that not every disability can be portrayed in each individual book, but as Melvin grows so will the number of titles available. Our hope in the future is to create more children's literature that can make all kids feel special and able to relate to.

If you have a title, or condition that you would like portrayed by the Melvin Books series, please contact us at contact@melvinbooks.com

Customizable areas within the book:

Pre-read the story and find areas that you feel your child could relate to better if you change the verbiage yourself. As an example, if your child is non-verbal and they communicate through sign language, with a computer or by simply listening to you and interacting in a different way, insert that method into the story instead of how Melvin communicates.

Melvin Goes to the Dentist

Sara Cremeno   Colleen Genest   Jonathan Coimbra

TINY HOUSE PUBLISHING (USA)

"Ahh," Melvin yawned. He rubbed his sleepy eyes while he walked to the bathroom. With his eyes still tired he reached around for his toothbrush and the forest-flavored toothpaste.

"Make sure you brush your teeth extra good today, Melvin!" Mama Moose hollered down the hall.

Melvin's antlers perked up and he poked his head out of the bathroom door, the toothpaste dripping from his mouth. "Why, Mama?"

"Today, you're going to see the dentist. Now, get brushing!" Mama said with a little pat on his head.

Melvin finished brushing his teeth and ran to find mama who was putting on her coat by the door.

"Are you ready, Melvin?" She asked, showing her sparkly white teeth as she smiled.

"But..." Melvin stuttered. He was really nervous about the dentist and he wasn't sure he wanted to go. "What will they do?"

"Today they are going to look at all of your teeth and count them to see how many you have. They have a special toothbrush that makes your teeth extra clean and sparkly. Why don't you hold my hand and we'll walk together. Today will be a fun day, Melvin." Mama Moose patted Melvin on the head again, rubbing the soft fur between his antlers. She gave his hand a little squeeze as they walked out of the house.

"Who's Dr. Bucky?" Melvin asked, pressing his feet into the dirt outside of the dentist's office.

"That's the dentist, Melvin. Come on, don't you want to know how many teeth you have?" Mama Moose asked, giving his hand a little tug.

Melvin thought about this for a moment and then tried to count his own teeth, but he kept loosing track. He wondered if he had more teeth than Mama Moose.

"Welcome. Have a seat and Olivia will be right out to get you." The lady smiled at Melvin and Mama Moose as they sat down in a corner filled with books and toys.

"Listen for your name, Melvin. They will call it when they are ready for us." Melvin rushed over to the toys as fast as he could.

(Parent's Guide: It's important to prepare your child that there will be a schedule and when their name is called it is their turn. A lot of kids have a hard time leaving the toys in the waiting room, but if they know they can come back to them, they normally find it easier. Inform your child that their name will be called when it is their turn and have them listen for it to stay alert and engaged.)

"Melvin?" Olivia opened the door and smiled as Melvin slowly raised his hand. She must have known he was nervous because she walked over and kneeled down by the toys with him.

"Hi, Melvin! I'm Olivia and I'm a dental hygienist. Is today your first visit to a dentist?" Melvin nodded. "Today is going to be really easy. If you come back with me you can pick a new toothbrush and we can count your teeth. Doesn't that sound fun?"

Melvin nodded again and looked over for his mom. "Don't worry, Melvin, Mama Moose is going to come with you so she can see how many teeth you have too. Would that make you feel better?" Melvin nodded and stood up. He started to feel a little excited about having his teeth counted.

(Parent's Guide: For your child's first few visits it's important to be there in the room. Your child will be looking for you for support and security, but keep in mind that the professionals have skills to help them complete their job and listening to their recommendations can make the appointment easier. Sometimes children do better on their own as they listen to the professionals, like they do their teachers and sometimes they will be better with you. If you think your child would do better on their own, discuss this with the dental hygienist and see what they think.)

Melvin walked with Olivia and Mama Moose until they reached a room with a really big chair.

"This is my really special chair, Melvin. It goes up and down. Would you like to go for a ride in mom's lap?" Olivia smiled at Melvin as he looked at the chair. It did look fun, he thought.

Mama Moose sat down in the chair and Melvin climbed up into her lap.

"Are you ready for a ride? 1...2...3!" Olivia made the chair move up towards the ceiling."Are you ready to go back down? Here we go!" Olivia brought the chair back down to the ground.

"Can we do it again?" Melvin asked.

"Of course. Want to try going by yourself this time?" Olivia asked. Melvin thought about it for a second and then nodded his head. Mama Moose stood up from the chair and let Melvin climb back up. Olivia made the chair rise higher than last time and Melvin laughed all the way to the top.

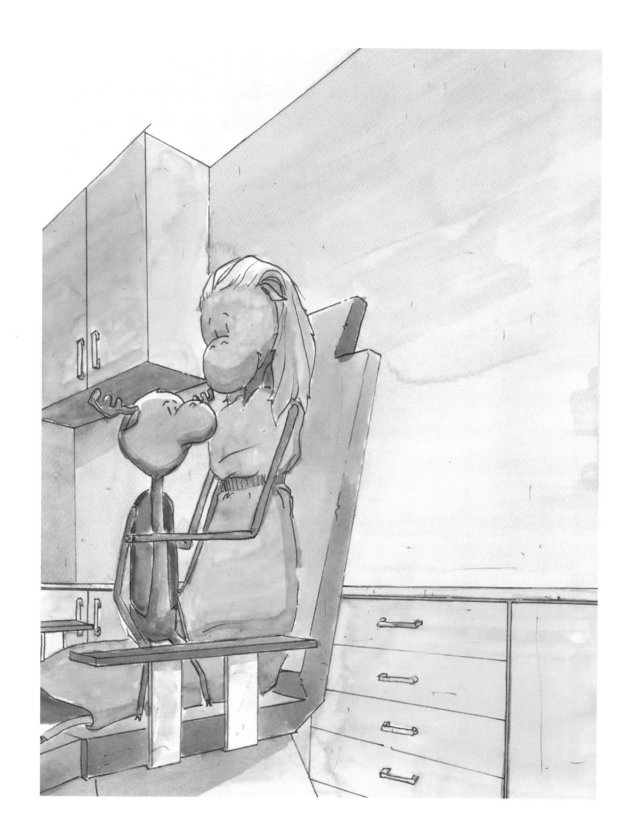

"What's next?" Melvin asked Olivia.

"Well, would you like to know how many teeth you have?" Olivia asked. He nodded quickly. "First, I'm going to show you my mask that I wear over my nose."

"Why do you need that?" Melvin asked. Olivia put on a white mask over her nose and mouth.

"This is so we don't share any coughs or sneezes." Melvin giggled at the thought of sharing a sneeze. "Now, I'm going to put on my water gloves. These keep my hands dry while I count your teeth."

"How do you count my teeth?" Melvin asked.

"I'm going to use my tiny tooth mirror. See?" Olivia held up a little mirror that could fit in Melvin's mouth. "Can you see yourself in the mirror?" Melvin nodded. "The last thing I need is my gentle tooth counter."

Olivia showed Melvin a tiny tooth counter and counted on her fingers.

"Let's see how big you can open." Olivia said. Melvin opened his mouth as wide as he could. "It's pretty dark in there. I'm going to turn on my special flashlight so I can see all of your teeth." Olivia turned on a light above Melvin and shined it into his mouth.

(Parent's Guide: For better success, practice opening wide at home. You can use an actual flashlight to look inside to simulate the overhead dental light. If you help prepare your child for what to expect before they go the better they will do. As you continue to read, practice the parts you can at home and discuss the parts you cannot.)

"That's better. Wow, I see a lot of teeth in here! Let's count. I see, 1, 2, 3, 4, 5, 6, 7, 8, 9, 10 on the top! And 1, 2, 3, 4, 5, 6, 7, 8, 9, 10 on the bottom! Do you know what 10 plus 10 is?" Melvin shook his head, no. "That's twenty teeth! That's a lot of teeth." Melvin smiled a big toothy smile at Mama Moose, who was watching him from her chair.

"Now, let's make those teeth nice and shiny." Melvin was excited now. He didn't know that he had twenty teeth and he wondered how shiny Olivia was going to make them. "This is my tickle toothbrush, Melvin. It spins and tickles your teeth just a little."

(Parent's Guide: Some children who have sensory processing disorder or other sensory concerns find that the toothbrush can be uncomfortable. Have a discussion with your child's dental hygienist before the appointment about the areas where your child can get uncomfortable. This will help the hygienist tailor the visit accordingly.)

"Would you like to feel it?" She held out a spinning toothbrush and showed him on her finger. Melvin held out his hand for the toothbrush. He let out a laugh as it tickled him.

"The light can be bright, Melvin. Would you like to wear some sunglasses today?" Melvin nodded and Olivia put a pair of sunglasses over his eyes.

(Parent's Guide: If you are unsure if your child's dental office has sunglasses available for the children, pack your own. The bright light can bother kids if they wiggle in their seat and sunglasses can help them feel comfortable and safe.)

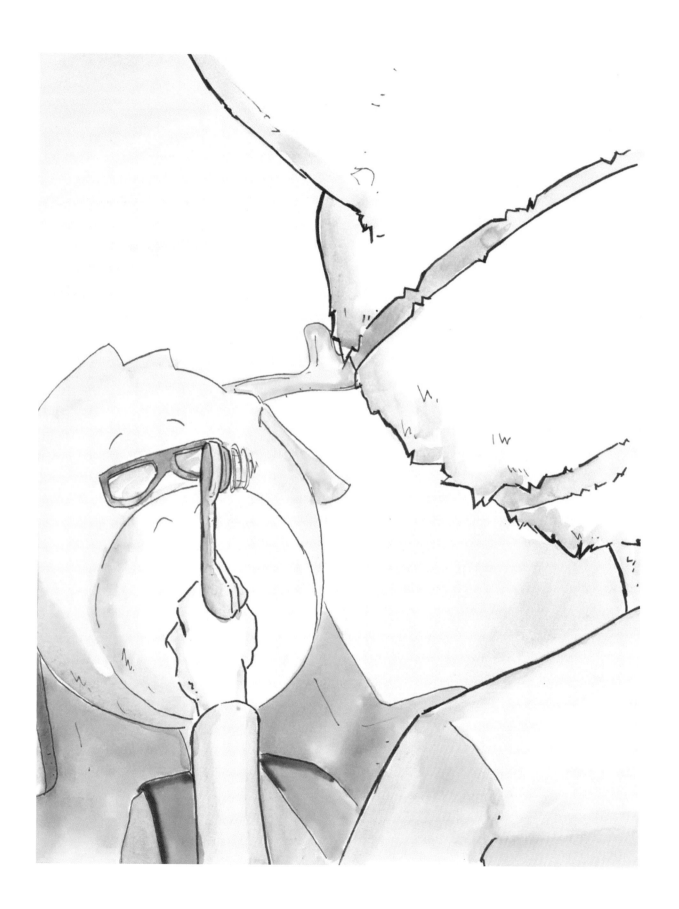

"Open really big and we'll brush all of your teeth so they're really shiny." Melvin opened as wide as he could and the flashlight shined in his mouth so Olivia could see. The toothbrush was soft and tickled just a little as Olivia brushed all twenty of his teeth.

"Does it feel a little sandy in there?" Olivia asked. Melvin nodded as he felt the sandy toothpaste with his tongue. "This is my water and thirsty straw. The straw makes a little noise when I turn it on and will vacuum up all of the water." Olivia showed him the water as she sprayed it into the straw.

"Open wide and I'll rinse all the sandy toothpaste out." Melvin opened as wide as he could and Olivia sprayed a little water over his teeth. "Now close your lips around the straw, Melvin." He did as he was told and the straw vacuumed up all the water. Olivia did this until all the toothpaste was gone.

"How does that feel?" Olivia asked.

"Much better!" Melvin said.

"Would you like to see how sparkly they are?" Melvin nodded as Olivia handed him a mirror.

"Wow!" Melvin said. They looked white and shiny and so clean!

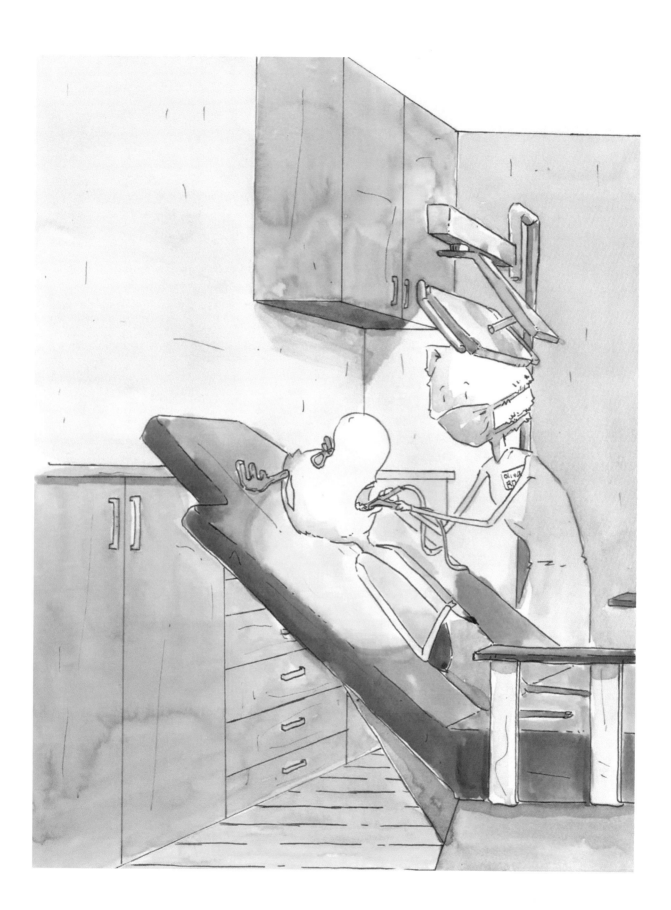

"The last thing we need to do is have Dr. Bucky count your teeth and make sure they're all healthy." Melvin thought about this for a second. He was a little nervous for someone else to check his teeth.

"Don't worry, Melvin. He's going to use the same mirror and tooth counter I used."

"Hi, Melvin. I'm Dr. Bucky. I heard you did a great job today. Let's check all those teeth and see how shiny Miss Olivia got them! Can you show me how big you can open?" Melvin opened his mouth for Dr. Bucky to check his teeth.

"That's great, Melvin. I'm just using the gentle tooth counter to check the top of all your teeth." Melvin opened his eyes after a moment. This was really easy, he thought.

"All done, Melvin. Thanks for being a great helper. Your teeth look nice and healthy and very shiny."

"You did such a great job today, Melvin! Would you like to pick out a new toothbrush to take home and a prize?" Olivia asked. Melvin nodded. He was so excited for a prize.

"Will you come back and see me again, Melvin?" Olivia asked as they walked out to the waiting room.

"Yes I will!" Melvin said as he gave her a big, toothy smile.

Going to the Dentist Survival Kit

- Pack sunglasses for the light if it gets too bright.
- Bring this book with you. If your child has learned and prepared through this text, let the hygienist read through it beforehand so they can try to use the same, familiar verbiage.
- Some children opt to watch a movie or a show on a tablet as they have their teeth cleaned and counted. If this sounds like something your child would like, pack it in case it's needed.
- Headphones are always a great idea, because the dental office can get noisy with children and equipment.
- Bring a special toy from home or something comforting for them to hold if needed. This may help reduce anxiety and stress and if asked the dental hygienist can count the plush toy's "teeth" first to make your child feel more comfortable.
- Medical offices can be a bit unpredictable. Bring something for your child to do in case there is a wait. This will help keep them distracted and help improve their success rate.

Going to the Dentist Survival Guide

- It's important to help prepare your child for the dentist in a kid-friendly way. Kids are very perceptive and it's important to avoid pushing any of your own dental anxiety onto them.
- Avoid sayings words such as, "hurt" or "shot." Children will instantly grab onto these words and focus on them. Instead of saying, "This won't hurt," try saying, "This will be really easy. The dentist is going to count your teeth and make them sparkly clean."
- Choosing the right dental office is key in having a successful visit. Ask your family and friends for referrals to a pediatric dental office that you'd feel comfortable bringing your child to.
- It's important for you and your child to feel comfortable and safe in the environment you choose. For the first few visits go back with your child. Once they are older and more comfortable it is up to you to decide as a family if you'd like to continue to stay in the room or let them try to be a bit more independent. Your hygienist will be happy to accommodate your choice to make it easy and successful for your child.

About the Authors

Sara Cremeno is a registered dental hygienist, working with a large population of special needs children at a pediatric dental practice. Sara spent three years before graduating college working for a dentist who focused his practice on treating special needs children and adults. She traveled to different facilities to treat patients in a variety of settings. Sara is also a contemporary young adult author.

Colleen Genest is the mother of three children, her youngest of which is autistic. She has spent many years advocating and educating in the community. She has worked closely with school professionals and Early Intervention through the years not only for her own child, but to help facilitate help for others. She also writes adult fiction books.

CPSIA information can be obtained at www.ICGtesting.com
Printed in the USA
BVIW12n1317121115
426523BV00001B/1